Cumbria Libraries

3 8003 04311 1046

KT-178-159

This Little Tiger book belongs to:

_____

_____

_____

For Jo and Mark ~ S P

LITTLE TIGER PRESS
An imprint of Magi Publications
1 The Coda Centre, 189 Munster Road, London SW6 6AW
www.littletigerpress.com

First published in Great Britain 2009
This edition published 2010

Text copyright © Magi Publications 2009 • Illustrations copyright © Simon Prescott 2009
Simon Prescott has asserted his right to be identified as the illustrator of this work
under the Copyright, Designs and Patents Act, 1988

A CIP catalogue record for this book is available from the British Library

All rights reserved • ISBN 978-1-84506-974-2

Printed in China

1 3 5 7 9 10 8 6 4 2

On A Dark Dark Night

Simon Prescott

LIBRARY SERVICES FOR SCHOOLS

38003043111046

Bertrams	17/05/2012
	£5.99
LSS	

LITTLE TIGER PRESS
London

In a dark, dark wood . . .

there was a dark, dark path.

Along the dark, dark path . . .

there was a dark, dark town.

In the dark, dark town . . .

there was a dark, dark street.

Down the dark, dark street . . .

there was a dark, dark gate.

Through the dark, dark gate . . .

there was a dark, dark yard.

In the dark, dark yard . . .

there was a dark, dark house.

In the dark, dark house . . .

there were some dark, dark stairs.

Down the dark, dark stairs . . .

there was a dark, dark room.

In the dark, dark room . . .

there was a dark, dark door.

And . . .

through the dark, dark door

there was . . .

. . . dinner!

Make a run for these Little Tiger Press books!

Small Mouse **BIG CITY**

Norbert Landa   Tim Warnes
Sorry!

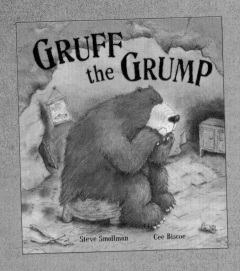

GRUFF the GRUMP

Steve Smallman   Cee Biscoe

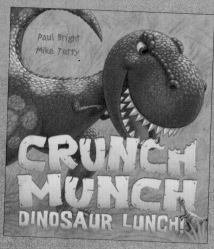

Paul Bright
Mike Terry

CRUNCH MUNCH DINOSAUR LUNCH!

Sylvia and Bird

Catherine Rayner

For information regarding any of the above titles or for our catalogue, please contact us:
Little Tiger Press, 1 The Coda Centre, 189 Munster Road, London SW6 6AW
Tel: 020 7385 6333 Fax: 020 7385 7333
E-mail: info@littletiger.co.uk www.littletigerpress.com